CHAPTER 1

#2

K. Harriel

CRITTERLAND ADVENTURES

LACTUS CACTUS

Story and pictures by Bob Reese

 CHILDRENS PRESS, CHICAGO

MY 30 WORDS ARE:

sun	itchy	desert
sand	on	hot
rose	my	and
feel	clothes	sticky
very	I	all
good	would	right
to	rather	okay
me	than	tingly
it	smell	in
is	a	nose

Library of Congress Cataloging in Publication Data
Reese, Bob.
  Lactus cactus.
  (Critter land adventures)
  Summary: A cactus gains a new appreciation of desert roses.
  [1. Cactus—Fiction. 2. Flowers—Fiction.
3. Stories in rhyme] I. Title. II. Series.
PZ8.3.R255Lac   [E]   81-3866
ISBN 0-516-02304-7   AACR2

Sun.

Sand.

Rose.

Sand feels very
good to me.

It is itchy
on my clothes.

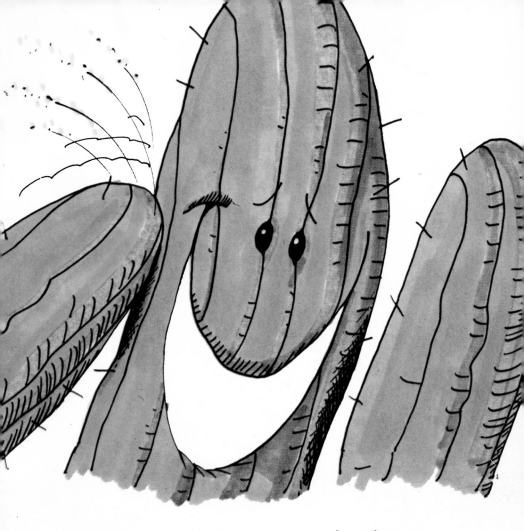

I would rather feel
itchy sand than . . .

than . . .?

than . . .?

Smell a desert rose.

Sun feels very
good to me,

hot and sticky
on my clothes.

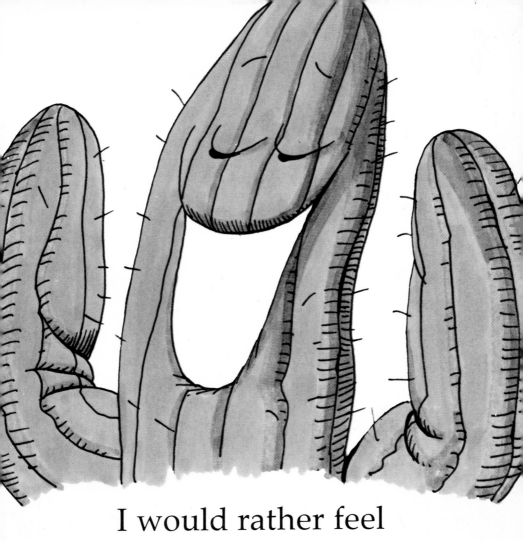

I would rather feel
hot and sticky sun
than smell a desert rose.

16

All right. Okay!

Roses smell very
good to me,

all tingly
in my nose.

I would rather smell
a tingly rose

than feel hot,
sticky, itchy clothes.

Bob Reese was born in 1938 in Hollywood, California. His mother Isabelle was an English teacher in the Los Angeles City Schools.

After his graduation from high school he went to work for Walt Disney Studios as an animation cartoonist. He received his B.S. degree in Art and Business and began work as a freelance illustrator and designer.

He currently resides in the mountains of Utah with his wife Nancy and daughters Natalie and Brittany.